Full Moon Stories

Stories

Thirteen Native American Legends

STORIES AND

ILLUSTRATIONS

BY EAGLE WALKING TURTLE

HYPERION BOOKS FOR CHILDREN
NEW YORK

Text ©1997 by Gary McLain.
Illustrations ©1997 by Gary McLain.

Printed in Hong Kong by South China Printing Company (1988) Ltd.

First Edition

1 3 5 7 9 10 8 6 4 2

3 1540 00176 6037

This book is set in 11.5-point Sabon with Bodega Sans display.

Designed by Learning Arts, Santa Fe, New Mexico.

Eagle Walking Turtle.
    Full Moon Stories/stories and illustrations by Eagle Walking Turtle.
       p. cm.
    Summary: Grandpa Iron tells thirteen stories, one for each full moon of the year, that convey some of the traditions and beliefs of Native Americans, particularly his Arapaho people.
    ISBN 0-7868-0225-1 (trade)—ISBN 0-7868-2175-2 (lib. bdg.)
    1. Arapaho Indians—Juvenile Fiction. [1. Arapaho Indians—North America—Great Plains—Fiction.] I. Title.
    PZ7.E118Fu 1997
    [Fic]—dc20   96-3462

contents

FOR GRANDPA IRON

WHEN I WAS A BOY I lived with my grandparents on the Northern Arapahoe Indian Reservation in Wyoming. Grandpa Iron was always happy and full of life's joy. Grandma Iron was much more serious. They both taught me, along with my brothers and sisters, that all of nature should be listened to, loved, and respected.

Each time a full moon came, Grandpa Iron would tell us a story. First he'd burn cedar needles, and we would fan the sweet-smelling smoke over our heads to purify our bodies before Grandpa's story. He always took his hat from the wall and placed it on the bed before he began his telling. I suppose this goes back to the time when warriors hung their medicine bags on the tipi pole behind them before speaking.

The following thirteen stories are among those that Grandpa told us about the love and respect our people have for our animal brothers and sisters—the four-leggeds, the ones that fly, the ones that slither in the grasses, and the ones that swim in the waters.

the magpie

IN THE MOON OF TREES POPPING IN THE WIND (January), Grandpa Iron told us kids a story about the magpie. My sister Betty and I had been running races, barefoot in the snow, with other kids that lived nearby, on the dirt road that ran over the hill past our house. There were not many cars on the reservation at that time, but I remember people used to get stuck on that road when it rained or the snow melted. They'd come in and drink coffee, waiting for the road to freeze back up.

When we saw the full moon rising, big and silver above the cold snow-covered plains, we ran into Grandma and Grandpa's log house and crowded around the big potbelly stove to get warm. We knew it was time for another of Grandpa Iron's stories. And we were real hungry.

When the sun went down, the road froze, and the people who had been stuck left. After supper, Grandpa Iron took his hat from the wall and laid it on the bed. We kids sat in a circle on the floor, and Grandpa smudged us off with sweet cedar smoke. Then he began a story about the magpie.

Once, a long time ago, the people were hungry; the tribe had no food. A chief called Red Lightning was out hunting one day when a big rain came and he took shelter in a cave and fell asleep. As he slept he dreamed that the Thunder-beings came to him and told him they would help his people. But first they wanted to know if the people were worth saving.

So the Thunder-beings told Red Lightning they were going to hold a race. The wings of the air and the two-leggeds of the universe would be on one side, and all the four-leggeds would be on the other. If the two-leggeds and the wings of the air beat the four-leggeds, they would be provided for. But if the four-leggeds won, they would eat the people and the birds.

Red Lightning was surprised at all the fierce four-leggeds who gathered for the race. And he was astonished at the number of brave warriors. The race started. The track ran clear around the circle of the Earth. The racers ran on and on. A big wind started to blow, so the magpie cleverly perched on a buffalo's ear and waited for the wind to die down. Later a hot day came; the buffalo could not run, so the birds pulled out in front. Then a big rain fell, killing some of the birds.

Again, the magpie rode out the storm on the buffalo's ear. With the racers almost around the Earth and the finish line in sight, the buffalo was in the lead. The four-leggeds cheered, each making the sounds it makes. Suddenly the magpie took to the air, flying high, then at once falling to the ground, faint with hunger and exhaustion. But he had crossed the finish just in front of the buffalo.

And that was how the wings and the two-leggeds won the great race. The Thunder-beings told the magpie always to wear a rainbow as a reminder of his victory, and indeed, his tail has a rainbow in it to this day. Then the Thunder-beings gave the bow and arrow to Red Lightning so he could hunt and provide for his people. And Red Lightning taught his tribe, so they had food and shelter from that time on.

Grandpa Iron told us that since that day the magpie has been our friend, respected because it was smart enough to win the race that saved our people.

Grandpa hung his hat on the wall, and Grandma passed around a dipper of cold water before tucking us under the big pile of quilts on the old iron bed. Grandpa turned out the lamp, and the wind blew a fine powder of snow through the cracks between the logs of the house.

We slept and dreamed of the great race that had saved the people.

And the Earth stayed young.

SECOND MOON

the horse

IN THE MOON OF GEESE COMING HOME
(February), Grandpa Iron told us kids about the horse. We were at the community hall, attending an honor dance for the men who had been in the United States armed forces. My uncle James had been a turret belly-gunner in a bomber and had flown many missions over Germany during World War II.

The afternoon was cold, and when the dance was over we went home to Grandma and Grandpa's house. Grandma put some dried meat in a canvas bag and we pounded it with a rock until the meat was in small pieces. Grandma added some salt for flavor. After our snack, Grandpa Iron went out for wood, and we sat in a circle around the woodstove, teasing each other and giggling. Sometimes there would be a fight, but Grandma always stopped us right away. None of us liked to be scolded by Grandma, so we tried to behave.

Anyway, when Grandpa came back in, he told us that tonight was the full moon. We all helped Grandma get supper and do the dishes, then sat quietly around the stove, waiting for Grandpa's story.

Grandpa took his hat from the wall and laid it on the bed. He turned down the lamp, and the dim light shadowed his face, emphasizing his rugged features. Grandpa's nose had been broken playing football at

9

Carlisle Indian School in Pennsylvania in the early 1900s. It had been crooked ever since. Jim Thorpe, a famous Indian athlete and one of the best American all-around athletes in history, had been at Carlisle at the same time.

After Grandpa cedared us off with smoke from the cedar needles he'd heated on the woodstove, he began his story about the horse.

A long time ago, the Cheyenne and the Kiowa moved south from the Black Hills. As they started their journey one of their medicine men had a vision about a four-legged animal. He told his people about it, but died soon after. Then one day two hunters went out looking for food. They found a spring and nearby the tracks of an animal they didn't recognize. They followed the tracks and came upon a horse with long hair on its neck and a long tail. They didn't know what it was. When they returned to the tribe, their chief told them to catch it with lariats made from rawhide. The hunters fixed a snare and soon caught the animal. Nobody knew what it was. Then they remembered the medicine man's vision. The people held a council and named the animal spirit dog, since it looked like a big dog. Because they had never seen a horse before, the people believed it was holy, a messenger from the Thunder-beings. But they were also afraid and kept it tied up. Then the horse had a colt, and everyone came to look. One day she made a funny noise, a nicker, and a stallion came to be with her. He was gentle also. The younger warriors began to ride him, and soon they found other horses, too. From then on our people had horses.

Grandpa Iron said the horse made our lives easier. Now we could hunt the buffalo and follow their herds. We could use the horse to pull our tipi poles and help move camp. They became our helpers and our friends. Our people became the best horsemen in the world. And horses are called spirit dogs to this day.

Grandpa took his hat from the bed and hung it back on the wall, signaling that the story was over. Grandma gave us mint tea in gray enamel cups. The cups were too hot to hold, and we had to set them on the floor to cool. After we drank our tea she tucked us into bed, and Grandpa blew out the light, singing softly a Sundance song.

We dreamed of riding fast with the wind on beautiful spotted horses.

And the Earth stayed young.

THIRD MOON

the dog

IN THE MOON OF BUFFALO DROPPING THEIR CALVES (March), the wind blew down the Wind River's canyons for days, subsiding only sometimes at night. We kids played outside and we ran with the wind, pretending to be wind spirits.

Late in the afternoon we saw the full moon rising, and we knew it was time for Grandpa Iron to tell us a story. We all ran to Grandma and Grandpa's house and helped Grandpa bring in the wood for the night's fire. After supper we helped Grandma with the dishes and sat on the floor around the stove, waiting for Grandpa's story.

Grandpa took his hat from the wall and laid it on the bed. After cedaring us off with the sweet cedar smoke, he started his story about how, a long time ago, a dog saved some of our people.

There was a man called High Eagle who was a good provider for his family. He had two daughters, one about thirteen years old and the other about three. One day High Eagle and his wife and daughters went together to hunt for food. They took their small dog and its four pups along with them. A short distance from the village they found a place with good grass for the horses and with good water, so they camped there. High Eagle hunted while his family stayed at the camp. High Eagle was a good hunter, and soon his family had plenty to eat. His wife dried lots of the meat to eat later. They were all enjoying themselves, camped by the little stream in their tipi.

One night High Eagle was tired and went to bed early. The dog and her pups slept nearby. High Eagle's wife and daughters stayed up. The little girl went outside the tipi to play, but before long she came in and asked for

13

something to eat. Then she went back outside. She did this several times. Suddenly ten enemy warriors walked into the tipi, uninvited. The little girl had been feeding them outside, not knowing that they were enemies. The meat had only made them hungrier and now they wanted more.

The family didn't know what to do. High Eagle invited his enemies to sit down, and he told his wife to feed them. After the men ate, they lay down to sleep, for they were very tired. High Eagle's wife got some red greasepaint and rubbed their feet with it, as was the custom. This made the enemies even more comfortable, and they slept hard.

Then the little dog got up and yawned. The younger girl said that the dog was talking. The dog said, "Take me and my little ones and run away or these men will kidnap us all." The little girl repeated to her mother and father what the dog had said . High Eagle went out and got the horses ready to leave. The older girl put the pups inside her dress, and the family started to sneak away while the enemies slept. High Eagle decided to make sure the enemies couldn't follow. He set the tipi on fire, then turned the enemies' horses loose. The family and the dogs all escaped safely.

Grandpa Iron said that the dog has always been good to our people.

Dogs are especially sacred to our people; some ceremonies are devoted only to them because of their loyalty and willingness to work.

Then Grandpa hung his hat back on the wall, and we drank the water that Grandma passed around to us in the white enamel dipper. After she tucked us into bed, we slept, dreaming of the time that the little dog saved a family.

And the Earth stayed young.

the moose

WHEN THE MOON OF ICE BREAKING IN THE RIVER (April) came, Grandpa Iron told us kids a story about the moose.

My sister Betty and I had been playing in the woods by the Wind River, throwing big rocks at the pieces of ice coming downstream, when we heard Grandpa Iron calling us. He was standing on the road that ran along the river, his wagon and team of horses close by. We sat on the back of the wagon, swinging our legs and watching the place we'd been get smaller and smaller.

Back home, Grandpa unharnessed the team and put them into our ramshackle corral. While Grandpa fed and watered them, we reached through the cracks in the fence to rub their legs and feel the soft hair on their bellies. Tufts of hair fell out and stuck to our fingers. The weather had been unusually warm, and the horses were beginning to shed already.

Later we ate our supper of beans and fry bread, looking outside at the full moon lighting up the misty Wyoming plains. We knew it was time for another story and hurried to help Grandma do the dishes and sweep the cabin floor. Grandpa Iron cedared us off with smoke and motioned for us to sit down. Then he laid his hat on the bed and began telling us a story about the moose.

Long ago, a band of our people was camped in a spot with lots of hot-water springs and natural fountains called geysers. Today that land is called Yellowstone National Park.

The chief of the band was a woman called White Wolf. White Wolf was good and kind at heart but given to fits of bad temper and loud yelling for even the slightest wrong. The people were beginning to wonder if they'd chosen the right person to be their leader. Some of the council began to meet secretly without her to talk about choosing a new chief.

15

The head of the council was a man called Small Bear. He had been struck by lightning some years before and had strong medicine powers as a result.

One day Small Bear was out alone, walking by a big lake that stretched halfway across the valley. He saw a bull moose in the crystal-clear water, grazing on the lake's bottom. A cow moose and her calf were standing on the shore watching the bull. Small Bear stopped behind a tree to observe. The big bull would graze on the lake's bottom for a few minutes, then wade out to stand by the cow and calf, then wade back in again to graze on the water plants. The bull was teaching the young calf how to obtain food.

Small Bear could not but admire the graceful, intelligent moose family and the gentle, patient way they communicated as they searched for food.

When Small Bear returned to his village, he called a special council meeting with White Wolf present. There he told the story of the three moose and what he had learned from them. White Wolf listened without her usual bad manners. Small Bear's medicine powers worked within him, and White Wolf realized the moose story was directed at her. She apologized to the council for her past rudeness, and her apology was accepted.

After that meeting, White Wolf was a different person. She was polite and considerate and always set a good example for her people. She remained chief until she died, an old woman.

Grandma scolded Grandpa for telling such a long story and he laughed out loud, like he always did when she scolded him. Then he hung his hat back on the wall. Grandma passed the leftover fry bread around and we sprinkled sugar on it so it tasted almost like doughnuts.

Grandma tucked us into bed with a good-night pat on the head for each of us, and Grandpa Iron blew out the coal-oil lamp.

We slept and dreamed of how good it must have been when we were wild and free.

And the Earth stayed young.

FIFTH MOON
the bear

IN THE MOON WHEN THE PONIES SHED THEIR SHAGGY HAIR (May), we kids were all playing down by the Little Big Wind River, which ran by the big log building that was our community hall. Grandpa Iron had been born many years before in a tipi not too far from the community hall. Of course no one lived in tipis anymore. They were used only for Native American Church meetings or for powwows or the Sundance.

Uncle Kail came by, stopping his old beat-up car just off the road. His yell brought us running. He said that there would soon be a full moon rising and that Grandpa Iron was getting ready to tell us a story about bears. We all piled in the car and rode to the small log house.

Grandma was out by the clothesline, taking down some wash that had dried in the warm May sunshine. Magpies had stolen some of the clothespins, and she was complaining to Grandpa when we walked up. He just laughed. Grandma glared at him.

Inside the cabin, we helped Grandma fold the wash and stack it on a shelf near the beds. Then Grandma started a stew of boiled dry meat with onions and potatoes. Baking-powder biscuits with butter and coffee made the meal complete. It was more food than usual for one meal, but I guess Grandpa had sold some scrap iron in town that day. After supper we did the dishes and Grandpa Iron smudged us off with cedar smoke. Then we sat on the floor, and he began his full-moon story.

A long time ago, when our people still lived in caves and walked everywhere, there was a medicine man called Moves Walking. Moves Walking had bear medicine power.

At that time, food was getting hard to find, so our people split into smaller bands, each band going in a different direction. Moves Walking was the leader of one band. He went into the wilderness to meditate and seek wisdom so he could take his people in the right direction. While seeking his vision he saw a family of bears gather in a grove of trees below the hill he was on. Moves Walking watched them for days. He watched the cubs play with each other and with their mother and father. He saw the mother bear discipline her young by cuffing their ears, and the father bear ignore them when he was tired or had other things on his mind. Moves Walking saw the roots, plants, and insects that the bears ate, many of which his people had thought inedible. He learned the roots and plants they ate when they were ill. After the bears left, Moves Walking went down the hill into their camp and found the remains of their food and medicine.

When Moves Walking went back to his people, he had a vision for the direction they should go, and he had the wisdom that the bears had taught him. From that time on, his name was Medicine Bear.

Grandpa Iron said that the bear medicine is good for people, too. A bear society was formed whose members have a great knowledge of healing. They know not only about roots and herbs for physical healing but also about healing mental conditions.

Grandpa took his hat from the bed and hung it on the wall. Uncle Kail laughed and waved good-bye as he went out the door and headed for home. The roar from his old car faded away as Grandma passed water around to each of us and turned back the covers on the iron beds. Grandpa blew out the coal-oil lamp after we were all tucked in bed, and the moonlight streamed through the cracks in the logs.

We slept and dreamed of the bear cubs playing in the trees.

And the Earth stayed young.

SIXTH MOON
the rabbit

IN THE MOON WHEN THE HOT WEATHER BEGINS (June), school let out. Betty and I were happy to have a vacation from school, but we missed some of the kids who we would not see again until Sundance time. A late snowfall covered the Wyoming plains, and we had fun having snowball fights with the kids who lived close by, but the snow lasted only one day. Then the warm June sun melted it and dried the mud that it left behind. Our melancholy returned.

To break our boredom Betty and I went with Uncle Kail to visit a friend that lived close to Dubois, and we stayed there for a while. The lady we were visiting had an old gray horse, and Betty talked me into riding it one day. I had to turn a bucket upside down on a chair to get on the mare's back. She wasn't the deadhead Betty and I thought she was! The mare ran away with me up a rocky streambed as far as she could go. I held tight to her mane but finally fell off to one side and landed in a pool of water that was too shallow to cushion my fall. The rocks really hurt, but Betty's laughing hurt me more. Still, Betty wouldn't even try to ride the old gray mare, so I decided that she couldn't make too much fun of me.

It was fun being on the little ranch by Dubois. The mountains nearby are beautiful. When Uncle Kail told us that it was time to

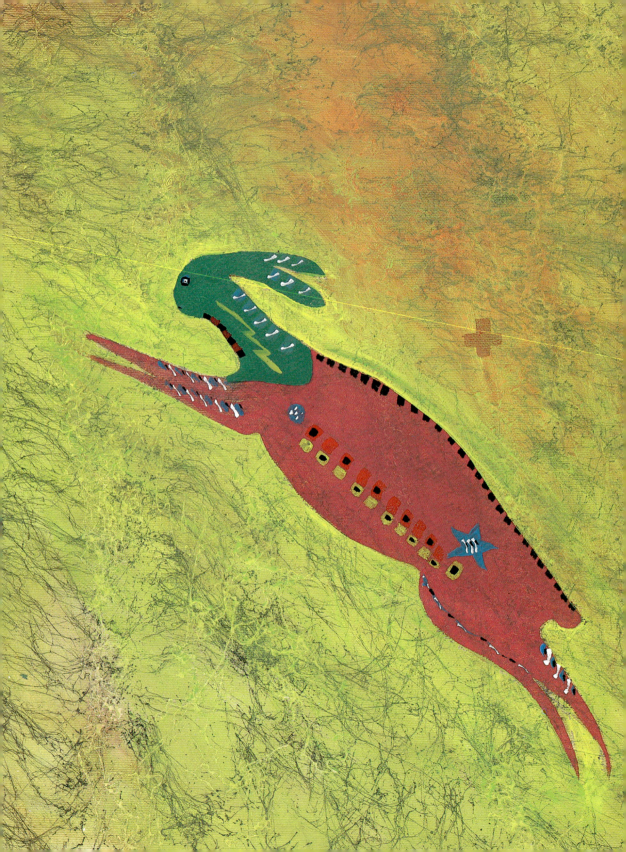

go home, we decided that we would visit the old lady at Dubois again someday.

The same night we got back home was the full moon. Grandpa told us right away that he was going to be telling a story about jackrabbits. After supper was over and our chores were done, Grandpa took his hat from the peg on the wall and laid it on the bed. We sat on the floor while he cedared us off with the sweet smoke and an eagle-feather fan. The smoke sure smelled good. Then Grandpa began his story.

Grandpa said that we have three lives: the first in the spirit world, then here on Earth, and then in the spirit world again. Twins are special, though. They live on the Earth not once, but four times. When it is time for them to be born again from the spirit world, twins, still in spirit form, must find a new mother by riding on the backs of jackrabbits. As soon as they find the mother of their choice, the twins wait for her to fetch water by the riverbank. After the spirits of the twins get inside their Earth mother, they develop into babies. When they are born and begin to talk, twins will tell you what the spirit world is like, and how they came to live on Earth again, riding jackrabbits.

Grandpa said that he himself had seen women waving their arms and yelling at jackrabbits when they went to get water at the river. They were trying to scare the rabbits away because they didn't want twin babies.

Grandpa laughed and we all laughed and clapped at his good story. It would be fun to ride on a jackrabbit. Then Grandpa hung his hat back on the wall and Grandma passed our water around before tucking us into bed. After Grandpa blew out the lamp, we lay in the soft darkness and fell asleep to dreams of riding horses and, of course, jackrabbits.

And the Earth stayed young.

the buffalo

IN THE MOON WHEN THE BUFFALO BELLOW (July), the days were hot and the nights were cold. Grandma and Grandpa Iron told Betty and me that it was time to load the wagon with our camp gear and move to the Sundance grounds for the annual ceremony.

We packed Grandma's old cavalry tent and a small wood cookstove we could use inside the shade house we constructed at the Sundance grounds. Lots of other things had to be packed: pots and pans, food, blankets and quilts, and the things each Sundancer needs, including eagle feathers, eagle-bone whistles, sweet sage, moccasins, bedrolls, and all the gifts the Sundancer would be giving away during the ceremony.

Grandpa was one of the old men that sit in the Sundance Lodge and help conduct the ceremony. Each Sundancer makes a sacrifice on behalf of all living things, going without food and water for four days so that all people and all life will stay in good health. The Sundance ceremony must be performed in the correct order; its preservation depends on passing on the oral teachings precisely to upcoming generations. Grandpa was teaching a younger man who would someday take his place. So we always were among the first ones to move to the Sundance grounds and among the last to leave. We were often camped there for ten days or more.

We roamed around the grounds wild and free, leaving the hard work of running the camp and conducting the ceremony to our elders. Our days were filled with playing and eating.

When the night of the full moon came, Grandpa Iron was at the big tipi in which the Rabbit Lodge Ceremony, the complete oral history of the

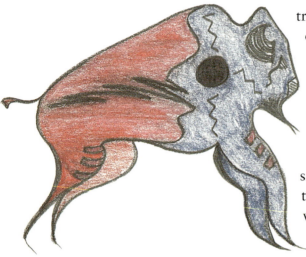

tribe, is conducted. He arrived back at our camp very late; the bright full moon hung in the thin clouds above the plains before he called us for our story. He placed some hot coals from the campfire in one of Grandma's skillets and sprinkled cedar needles on them. Sweet smoke filled the air, and we all took turns smudging ourselves off. Then we sat to listen.

He took the hat from his head and held it on his lap as he began to talk. Grandpa said that his grandfather's grandfather told him that his grandfather's grandfather could remember when the people first met the buffalo on the Great Plains of what is now America. They already knew of the buffalo from the story the old people told of the time when the magpie beat the buffalo in the great race. Now after the race, the buffalo gave himself to the people for meat; he gave his hide for tipis; and many other things he gave so that our people's lives could be easier. For hundreds of years Plains Indians followed the migration of the buffalo herds and depended on them for food and shelter. When the buffalo were almost exterminated because of unchecked and wasteful hunting by non-Indian settlers, it was the end of our people living wild and free.

Grandpa said that we still place a buffalo's hide in the crook of the Sundance Tree as our thanks for the many good things that the buffalo did for our people. The buffalo is sacred—among all living things, one of the most important.

Grandma Iron passed around cups of hot stew and fry bread to everyone, and Grandpa said a prayer giving thanks for the food. After supper we crawled into our beds and listened to the heartbeat of Grandmother Earth, the Sundance drum, and the cries of the eagle, our Father Sky, from the Sundancers' whistles. I floated above the ground, dreaming of the good times, when our people followed the buffalo herds.

And the Earth stayed young.

EIGHTH MOON
the owl

IN THE MOON WHEN THE CHOKECHERRIES BEGIN TO RIPEN (late July), we moved our camp from the Sundance grounds to the powwow grounds for the big seven-day-long celebration that says we had had a good Sundance. Betty and I helped load the wagon and sat on the back for the short trip. Some of the other kids ran alongside, and we laughed and giggled all the way. After we helped unload and set up the new camp, Betty and I ran off to play while Grandma fixed a meal for us. Grandpa Iron had told us that another full moon would be rising soon, about when the powwow ended, and that he would be telling us a story about the owl.

So we danced and played with the other kids at the powwow. All the dancers in their colorful costumes made us feel happy to be at this social gathering. Each afternoon and evening and far into the night the big drum sounded out our people's love affair with all natural things. The drum's beat represents the heartbeat of our Grandmother Earth. The strong sound is a reminder, reassuring us that she is always there.

The warm days passed by quickly, and on the final day of the powwow it was time to load the wagon and move back home. Grandpa Iron said that our full moon story would be told that night, so we hurried to help with the move, and we ran alongside the wagon, sometimes jumping on the back to ride, and then jumping off again to play with the other kids that ran along with us.

Once home, we unloaded the wagon and helped Grandma fix our supper. After dinner I was out gathering wood for the cookstove when I saw the moon rising above the sagebrush-covered plains. I hurried to help

Grandma with the dishes while Betty swept the floor. Then we ran down the road to the neighbors to borrow a tool that Grandpa needed. On the way home a spirit followed us, its voice strange-sounding in the still night air. It was talking in Indian but we still couldn't understand what it was saying; probably it was in the old tongue that our people spoke many years ago. It sure scared us. We ran fast to get back to the house. No sooner had we gotten inside and slammed the door shut than a thump sounded from something hitting the house. Grandpa looked out and in the moonlight he saw a huge owl sitting in a nearby tree. And at the bottom of the door, on the step, were a set of deer antlers. Grandpa said that the owl had thrown the antlers against the house. He said that the owl was warning us to pay attention and treat all life better. When we told him about the spirit voice, he said that it, too, was the owl.

Grandpa got us all together and cedared us off right away. He took his hat from the wall, placed it on the bed, and started his story.

At one time a band of our people were camped for the winter on the Sweetwater River. A young woman died suddenly in an unexplained manner. Then more young women died, one after another. Each time one of the women died, her body was placed on a scaffold and wrapped tightly in a buffalo robe. One morning a relative of one of the dead women was mourning at the scaffold on which the body rested when she noticed that the head of the dead woman was unwrapped. When she looked at the dead woman's face, she was terrified to see that the deceased's mouth was open and her tongue was gone.

After examining other bodies on the scaffolds, the people discovered that those bodies, too, had missing body parts. Everyone, including the medicine men, thought that someone from the village was stealing the body parts.

The daughter of a wealthy chief died soon after and she was placed on a scaffold with all her life's treasures. Before long her tongue was stolen— but none of the treasures. So a man from the camp volunteered to watch the scaffolds all night to see what was going on. In the middle of the night he heard an owl hooting. Somehow it sounded like a person. In the moonlight he saw a big bird flying. It landed in a small pine tree. But when he looked closer, he saw a man in the tree, not a bird. How could a man fly like that? Pretty soon the man flew to a body on a scaffold and began to unwrap it. The man from the camp asked the birdman what he was doing. The birdman said that he was gaining the power to fly from the dead one's body parts, and the power to take the shape of an owl.

The man from the village killed the birdman and ran to tell all those in the nearby camps what had happened. They built a big fire and examined the birdman's body. He was dressed like a medicine man and carried small bundles around his neck of things from the bodies he had bothered. The village chiefs decided that he should be burned, so the birdman's body was thrown in the fire. By the next morning there was nothing left of him at all. And the unexplained deaths in the village stopped completely. Grandpa said that owls can be good medicine, but they can also be the messengers of impending death. Because they work and play in the dark night, they will always remain a mystery to us. Still, like all living things, they deserve our respect.

Grandpa Iron hung his hat back on the wall and Grandma gave us our drink of water before bedtime. After we were all snuggled in our beds in the darkness, the owl hooted once from the nearby tree.

And the Earth stayed young.

NINTH MOON

the mole

WHEN THE MOON OF GEESE SHEDDING THEIR FEATHERS (August) came, Grandma and Grandpa Iron left us kids with Uncle James so they could go out into the plains to pick up bones and scrap iron with the team and wagon. Grandpa sold the bones to a fertilizer plant, and he sold the iron to a scrap yard in Riverton.

Uncle James was good to us and always took time to tell us stories and take us to town for a special treat. The first time I ate popcorn was with Uncle James when I was eight years old. It is still one of my favorite snacks.

When Grandma and Grandpa returned home, Uncle James took us back to their house. He stayed to have coffee with the old folks. Whenever someone visits an Indian home, they are expected to stay for food or at least coffee. It is an insult to the host if the guest does not accept his hospitality.

That night after supper Grandpa Iron was talking to Grandma about the old days, when they were young. Grandma pretended that she wasn't interested, but when Grandpa started teasing her about how they had met, I saw a tear in her eye. They'd met at a powwow social dance when they were both very young; Grandpa had given her an eagle feather. Anyway, she just brushed the tear away and busied herself with some chore that did not need to be done right away. I knew then that she was a lot softer inside than she pretended to be.

31

Grandpa laughed out loud as he took the leather pouch that held his cedar needles out from under the bed. Grandma heated the cast-iron skillet on the cookstove and Grandpa sprinkled some needles into it to make the sweet cedar smoke for smudging us off. Then he placed his hat on the bed and we all sat down to listen to our full-moon story.

In the days before our people had to live on reservations and stay in one place, there was a brave warrior called Crazy Horse. He was a great Lakota leader, but he was not a chief or a medicine man. Grandpa said he led our warriors against the soldiers in a famous battle on the Greasy Grass River (the Little Big Horn). The battle was a great victory for our people, but it still didn't save our way of life. The American government's relentless policies toward Native American people eventually forced all our people onto reservations.

Crazy Horse had mole medicine, Grandpa said. Crazy Horse could appear in battle, and then disappear, only to appear again someplace else— like the mole. His medicine power kept him safe from bullets fired by the enemies' guns. He would ride out in front of his warriors in battle to taunt the enemy, but he was wounded only once and it was a minor wound. Grandpa Iron said that, like the mole, Crazy Horse was humble and quiet. He was generous as well, giving food and gifts and horses to anyone in need. He wore one single eagle feather and his hair was worn loose, except for special occasions.

We have great respect for this man, Crazy Horse, because he cared so much for our people and worked so hard to keep us free. Grandpa said that Crazy Horse was stabbed in the back and killed by Indian policemen that were working for the United States Army. No picture was ever made of him and his body was buried in a secret place that is still secret to this day. Grandpa said that because he will never be forgotten, his spirit lives on with us.

When Grandpa finished his evening prayer, he hung his hat back on the wall and Grandma tucked us into bed and blew out the lamp. The moonlight streamed through the cracks in the cabin wall and tiny warriors on horseback rode through the air in the smoke from Grandpa's cedar smudge.

And the Earth stayed young.

the coyote

IN THE MOON OF DRYING GRASS (September), Betty and I were glad that school was starting again. We were happy to see friends we hadn't seen since the powwow. We walked to school down a dirt road and across the highway, about a mile, I guess. The school was operated by a church mission. The nuns wouldn't allow us to speak Indian at school, only English. If we were caught talking in our own language, the nuns would hit us on our hands with a ruler. Today the mission schools are teaching the Indian language to kids and trying to bring back traditions that they tried to destroy when I was young.

One day after school let out, Uncle Kail came by in his old car to pick us up. We were glad to get a ride home. Uncle Kail said that Grandpa Iron was ready to tell us our full-moon story, right after supper.

So we hurried to do our chores and Grandma did the dishes so Grandpa could get right to our story. As the full moon rose Grandpa cedared us off and placed his hat on the bed. Then he began to tell us about the coyote.

Somewhere near the Powder River there was a man from our tribe called White Smoke. One day he left his village to go hunting for food. Only a short distance away he ran into a coyote. This was very unlucky, because the coyote is known to be a tricky, troublemaking creature. He can change shape, and he can make other people and animals follow his wishes. As soon as he saw White Smoke, he tricked him into fainting.

When White Smoke came to, he crawled to a nearby badger hole. At first the badger wouldn't let him enter, but finally he welcomed White Smoke in and doctored him with red willow, sage, and cedar. Even so, he still

34

was quite ill from the coyote's trick. A grasshopper brought him some medicine roots, and soon White Smoke began to feel stronger.

Meanwhile the coyote had traveled to White Smoke's tipi, pretending to be White Smoke. White Smoke's wife and older son believed that the coyote was their husband and father and accepted him. But the younger son did not, younger children having more insight.

When White Smoke had recovered, the badger told him to go home. On the way, White Smoke heard someone talking to him. It was an eagle, telling him to go west. So White Smoke went west toward the Big Horn Mountains, and there he met a crow. The crow told him to go to the Wind River. Even though he knew that the crow was a friend of the coyote, and perhaps part of the coyote's plan, he followed the crow's directions. Sure enough, he found no sign there of what to do. Some fish spirits there, who had also been tricked by the coyote, sent him into the desert and further confused him.

Finally, with the help of a buzzard, White Smoke returned to the Wind River and followed it south, where he found his tipi. Since the coyote had changed White Smoke's appearance, neither his wife nor his older son recognized him. The younger son, of course, knew him at once.

That night, when the coyote returned to the tipi, he was surprised to find White Smoke with his family. He cunningly asked White Smoke to help him find feathers to make better arrows to use for hunting food for his family. White Smoke foolishly agreed, and they climbed up to an eagle's nest. The nest was high up on a cliff. White Smoke asked the coyote to go up the steep cliff first, but the coyote refused, so White Smoke led the way. When he reached the nest, perched on a jagged rock, he saw that there were no feathers there, just large black locusts. The coyote had gotten the best of him once more. The coyote came up behind him and blew the nest and the rock, with White Smoke dangling from it, into the sky. Then he started on his way back down to White Smoke's tipi, confident that White Smoke would never bother him again.

An eagle who had seen what the coyote was up to decided to help White Smoke. But while he was flying off to get help, a lightning bolt struck the nest and White Smoke mysteriously disappeared.

Suddenly White Smoke found himself back at his very own tipi. Again, his younger son recognized him and warned him that the coyote would soon be back. White Smoke immediately told his wife, who finally knew her true husband, to grind chokecherries with poisonous rocks into a delicious-looking dish for the coyote to eat.

When the coyote entered the tipi, White Smoke spoke up right away and told him to have some of the chokecherry gravy his wife had made. The coyote agreed, feeling sure that he was a much smarter creature than White Smoke.

As soon as the coyote ate the poison rocks in the chokecherry gravy, he ran around the fire, crying that his belly was hurting. Then he fell down and begged White Smoke to help him. But White Smoke refused—he had been tricked for the last time. So the coyote died right there in the tipi. He would never cause trouble again.

Grandpa laughed and put his hat back on the wall peg. Grandma scolded him for telling such a long story and he laughed again. Then we had our drink of water and Grandma tucked us into bed and blew out the lamp.

A coyote howled way off out in the plains.

I thought about how we kids often tricked each other in fun, but how sometimes it is not good to trick anyone, even in fun, because it can cause hurt feelings or lead to big trouble.

And the Earth stayed young.

ELEVENTH MOON

the swallow ·

WHEN THE MOON OF FALLING LEAVES (October) came, Betty and I were doing well in school. The English language was confusing to us, but we had finally learned enough to read the books that the nuns sent home with us. Now we were reading stories to Grandma and Grandpa.

On the night of the full moon Grandpa cedared us off and laid his hat on the bed. While Grandma did the supper dishes Grandpa Iron told us a story about swallows.

There once was a band of people that lived in a place south of us. They were called the swallow people because they built their homes in cliffs. This place was safe from enemies because it was difficult to climb up to and hard to get down to from above.

Grandpa Iron said that swallows make their nests in the cliffs side by side, safe from predators, but each nest has its own narrow opening. So the people built their homes much like the swallow. And, like the swallow, they kept busy gathering food and water, raising their families, and enjoying the goodness of life.

But once in a while a child would be born who was afraid of the high place where the swallow people lived. Their families wondered what to do. Even the medicine people couldn't find a cure.

So the elders were consulted. After long council meetings it was decided that those people who were afraid of high places could live in the valley below and help with the cultivation of crops and anything else that needed tending.

So as soon as the children who were afraid became old
        enough, they were carried down the ladders, and homes
        were built for them in the valley.
                At first the homes were made from brush, sticks, and
                boughs of trees, and covered with animal
        skins. Later stones and poles were used. The valley
        people developed their own culture, different from
        that of the cliff people. But they were still close
        neighbors, the same people really, and their
ceremonies to give thanks to all living things were similar. Sometimes the
valley people would even find the courage to climb up the ladders to
participate in a ceremony in the cliffs.

    The valley community grew in numbers, while the cliff community
stayed about the same. And some of the cliff people started to resent how
well the valley people were doing. They saw that the valley people enjoyed
an easier life with fields, water, and game close by and without the hard
work of climbing ladders to come and go. And since the valley people had
less work to do, they had more time for ceremonies, craftwork, the arts,
and social activities. Eventually everyone moved into the valley, abandoning
the cliff homes above.

    But they had forgotten the reason they'd built their homes in the cliffs
in the first place. One day a large number of enemy warriors invaded the
valley village and stole the people's food and even kidnapped some of the
men, women, and children. They should have remained in the cliffs after all.

    So the remaining villagers moved back into the cliffs and lived safely
again. The valley village was abandoned and the people never again forgot
the swallows' medicine powers, which kept them high and safe and secure.

    Grandpa Iron said that we should never lose sight of our original goals
even if things in life become hard.

    Grandma passed around our water in the white enamel dipper, and we
crawled into our beds. Grandpa blew out the lamp while he sang the
evening Sundance song.

    And the Earth stayed young.

TWELFTH MOON

the deer

IN THE MOON WHEN THE RIVERS START TO FREEZE (November), Betty and I went to the Thanksgiving Day powwow with Uncle James. The community hall was packed with people and dancers, so some of the food for the feast was being cooked outside in huge cast-iron pots over open fires. Long tables were set up, piled high with fry bread, cookies, salads, fruits, and chokecherry gravy. We filled our bowls with stew from the pots and sat in the sun, eating until we thought we would burst.

I remember that there were so many dancers they had to line up outside the hall for the grand entry that began the powwow. At the head of the line, Uncle James and other veterans carried the American flag, the Wyoming flag, and banners representing all the Indian nations.

That night after the powwow was over and we were back home, Grandpa said it was time for our full moon story. Grandma gave us some stew and fry bread left over from the powwow feast, and then Grandpa cedared us off, laid his hat on the bed, and started his story about the deer.

One day a fawn heard the Great Spirit calling to her from the top of a sacred mountain. She immediately started up the rough mountain trail. The fawn didn't know that a bad spirit, one of many who live on Earth, guarded the way to where the Great Spirit lives. The bad spirit was trying to keep all living things from communicating with the Great Spirit. If he succeeded, he would feel even more powerful than the Great Spirit.

But the fawn was not frightened when she encountered the bad spirit. This was very strange because the bad spirit was the image of every bad thing anyone has ever seen. The bad spirit tried to scare the fawn by

blowing fire and smoke at her and making loud noises. It seemed as if the fawn should have run away or died on the spot from fear.

But the fawn did not. She said, very gently, to please let her pass so she could visit the Great Spirit. Her eyes were filled with love and sorrow for the bad spirit.

The bad spirit was surprised by the fawn's lack of fear. No matter how hard he tried, he could not frighten the fawn, because her love had filled his ugly, hardened heart.

The bad spirit's heart began to melt, and his body shrank to the size of an acorn. The fawn's love and gentleness had caused the bad spirit to shrivel and almost completely disappear.

Grandpa said that because of the fawn, the path has always been open for all living things to communicate with the Great Spirit. No bad spirits will ever be in our way again. The Great Spirit's love is always available for anyone in pain or seeking peace.

Grandma motioned for us to climb in bed after we had our drink of water. Grandpa blew out the lamp. We slept and dreamed of the sacred mountain where the Great Spirit lives.

And the Earth stayed young.

43

the turtle

WHEN THE MOON OF POPPING TREES (December) came to the Wind River, it was holiday vacation and Betty and I were home every day. It was good to be out of school for a while, but Grandma made us do more chores than usual, so it wasn't long before we wanted to go back. To make matters worse, the weather had turned bad. The wind was blowing the snow so hard that we couldn't even play outside.

Then the full moon rose above the cold and windy Wyoming plains. Betty and I had been outside helping Grandpa feed the horses when we saw it rising. The moon was red and big, with huge snow-filled clouds blowing across it. When it came up higher, it turned silver and cold like the wind.

After we got wood in for the stove, Grandma fixed supper and we helped do the dishes and clean the cabin. Grandpa cedared us off and Grandma wrapped blankets around us as we sat around the woodstove. Then Grandpa laid his hat on the bed and started his telling of a story about the turtle.

A long time ago, before our people lived in tipis and even before they met the buffalo, our people lived on a big island in a place that was always warm. Things were good; life was happy and food was easy to find. But because life was easy, the tribe's population grew, and it was not long before there were too many people for too little food. People began to find less and less to eat and they started to fight over the food that was available.

Anyway, one day a man named Red Hawk was watching turtles in a creek that ran into the ocean near his home. Red Hawk wondered why there was always plenty for the turtles to eat and why the number of turtles living in the creek never seemed to grow.

So Red Hawk marked a young turtle's shell with a white **X** and watched this turtle for days and days. Finally, one day the turtle with the white **X** swam toward the ocean. Red Hawk followed. When the turtle entered the open sea, Red Hawk followed in his boat. All day he followed the turtle. At last, just as the sun was setting, the turtle and Red Hawk reached a new land, with trees, water, and plenty of game for hunting. The few people there were very friendly.

Well, Red Hawk went back home in his boat right away to tell his people what he had found. Everyone rejoiced. The new land meant that everyone could live with plenty of food and without quarreling. Many of Red Hawk's tribe loaded their families and goods into boats and moved to the new land to live. Red Hawk was a hero, and the turtle was, from that time on, special for our people.

Grandpa said that we can learn from the turtle, who is slow but deliberate. We, too, should be patient and should always stop to think before acting.

Grandpa hung his hat back on the wall and Grandma passed around the water dipper. As Grandma tucked us into bed and blew out the lamp, Grandpa sang the song of Grandmother Earth. And I remember dreaming of the love and goodness of Grandmother Earth, our turtle.

And the Earth stayed young.

GRANDPA IRON taught us kids to always make room—in our hearts and on the Earth—for all living things. He told us never to forget that our existence and coexistence with the animals that share our planet depend upon our love and understanding. Without them, we are lost.

These thirteen full moon stories came and went, and thirteen more followed each year until I left the reservation, a grown man and living on my own. I remembered many of the stories and taught them to my children, and their children, passing on as I did so the traditions of my people of peace, love, and harmony with the world around us.